THE CHEEKY CAT
meets the QUEEN

Written by Rippon Pawa

Illustrated by Amy Harwood

To
Zeta and Zara
Happy Christmas 2018
Stay Cheeky!!
Love Masan

For Amiya
and Nikhil

Once upon a time, there was a cat called

GINGER.

Ginger loved pretending to be a Cat Princess
with her best friend Mia, the little girl who lived next door.

Ginger had always dreamed of meeting the Queen of
England, but never thought she would have the chance to.

One day Mia, her brother Nicky and her Mummy and Daddy, decided to take a trip to London to see the Palace, where the Queen lived.

Ginger thought,

"this might be my chance to meet the Queen"

So when Mia's Mummy and Daddy weren't looking,
Ginger jumped into the back of the car to go with them.

When they got to the Palace, Ginger
quietly jumped out of the car.

As Ginger was taking a walk, she saw that the front door of the Palace was open.

This is my chance to meet the Queen

she thought.

When Ginger saw nobody was looking, she started...

running, running, running, running,

to the front door and got one paw inside the door, when suddenly a tall soldier jumped out and said:

GINGER,
you cheeky cat!

You aren't allowed
in the Queen's Palace.
Before the Queen sees you, you
better turn around and go back!

So Ginger turned around
and went back to the car.

Later that day, as Ginger was wondering around outside the Palace, she saw the Palace window was open.

When Ginger saw nobody was looking, she started...

running, running, running, running,

to the open window and got
one paw,
then two paws
inside, when suddenly another Soldier
jumped out and said:

GINGER,
you Cheeky Cat!

You aren't allowed
in the Queen's Palace.
Before the Queen sees you, you
better turn around and go back!

So Ginger turned around
and went back to the car.

A few hours later, Ginger went for
another stroll, when she saw the
back door was open to the Palace.

When Ginger saw nobody was looking, she started...

running, running, running, running,

to the back door and got

one paw,
then two paws,
then three paws

inside the door, when suddenly another
Soldier jumped out and said:

"GINGER,
you Cheeky Cat!

You aren't allowed in the Queen's Palace.
Before the Queen sees you, you better
turn around and go back!"

So Ginger turned around and went back to the car.

It was now getting late.

Although Ginger really wanted to meet the Queen, she thought about being a good cat and just waiting for Mia and her family to come back to the car so she could go home.

BUT THEN....

Ginger looked up and saw the front door to the palace was open again.

Let me try to meet the Queen one more time

she thought.

So Ginger went very slowly at first and when nobody was looking, she started…

running, running, running, running,

This time Ginger got
one paw,
then two paws,
then three paws,
and finally four paws
into the front door.

THE CHEEKY CAT HAD
MADE IT INTO THE PALACE!!!!

A soldier then jumped out
and was just about to tell
Ginger to leave when...

...the Queen came down the stairs and saw her!

Oh what a delightful little cat, would you like some milk, Ginger?

the Queen asked.

Ginger couldn't believe it, the Queen of England knew her name.

Ginger, being the Cheeky Cat she was, ran straight to the kitchen and jumped onto the Queens lap to drink some milk.

The Queen was so used to playing with her dogs, she had forgotten how much she loved cats.

As the Queen was having so much fun, she asked Ginger to come for a tour around the Palace.

Ginger loved being stroked by the Queen and really enjoyed walking around the Palace, seeing all the beautiful things.

Ginger was enjoying herself so much, she almost forgot she had to leave with Mia to get back home.

After giving one last cuddle to the Queen, Ginger ran to the car.

Ginger saw Mia and her family were getting ready to leave, so she jumped into the back seat and cuddled up with Mia.

On the journey home, Ginger slept all the way and dreamt about being a Cat Princess living in that big Palace.

Ginger really was a
Cheeky Cat!!!

Rippon Pawa

This is my second book, following on from *The Cheeky Cat* in 2014. I was not sure whether I should write a second book but then I always felt that Ginger had a few more cheeky stories still to tell, so thought why not (my kids asking me to write a second book on an almost daily basis also played a part!!!). I hope you and your little ones enjoy this story as much as I enjoyed writing it. Stay Cheeky!

Amy Harwood

I'm an Illustrator and Blogger from Southampton, UK. I work by the sea in my home studio that I share with my bunny, Charlie. In my spare time I enjoy reading, writing and exploring. My favourite things to draw are animals, plants and dinosaurs. Check out my work at amyharwood.com!

Other titles from the author:

The Cheeky Cat